muse.

grey huffington

thank you.

wow.

25.

who would've thought?

twenty-five books in less than 3 years.

i'm grateful, for your support and for my will.

it's not always easy, but i continue to get it done.

i can't force myself to apologize for not giving you more this year.

honestly, truly… i had nothing to give.

but, lucky you…

fall is my favorite season.

winter keeps me inside.

both, in which, will result in random releases from me.

some shorter than others.

some long.

depends on where my pen ends.

nevertheless, i'm in love with this story.

i'm in love with these characters.

if you've ever been afraid of love…

afraid of life…
this one is for you.

g.

p.s. love you tons.

CLUB GREY

Are you ready to be apart of Club Grey where you will receive exclusive updates, read unpublished stories that are ONLY for club members, get $$ off purchases and keep up with all things Grey Huffington?
Well, here's your chance.
Did I mention you can win prizes?

TEXT 'greyhuffington' to 900900

LET'S CONNECT

Have you followed me on Instagram to stay updated with the latest on Grey?
Click below to follow.
Instagram
@greyhuffington
(www.instagram.com/greyhuffington)

Join my READING GROUP on Facebook!
"All Grey Everything"

I've launched my new website. Visit and discover all the goodies I have waiting for you!
VISIT ME ONLINE
www.greyhuffington.club

DISCLAIMER

This work of fiction contains explicit sexual content and is only intended for mature readers. **Do not turn another page if you are faint-hearted and can't withstand steamy, hot sex scenes.** This piece contains many sexual encounters in which are very unconventional. This piece also contains explicit adult language, occurrences, situations and decisions that may offend some readers.

To all others, enjoy!

Muse.

Inspired by @sew_trill – my favorite artist (painter) on Earth – and @sza – my favorite creator on Earth.

*And, **to my grandfather**, a hero and the true definition of a man. **You're not fighting your battle alone**. I'm here, even when I'm not there. I love you and evidence of our love will live forever in between these pages.*

g.

muse.

grey huffington

ONE

sew sidora

THIS TIME next year I'll be livin' so good
  Won't remember your name, I swear
  Livin' so good, livin' so good, livin' so good
  This time next year I'll be livin' so good
  Won't remember no pain, I swear
  People got you figured out, I was just a normal girl

SZA HAD SUCCESSFULLY COORDINATED the soundtrack to my life. My horrible attempts to harmonize with the vocal goddess filled me with first-hand embarrassment. Still, I sang as my life depended on it because once upon a time, it did. Once upon a time, it was the very song that I was singing that got me through long, agonizing hours in the oncology center. Around that time last year, I sang this portion with the confidence that it would come to fruition and I'd be living so damn good that I didn't remember the pain.

But, it was impossible. I remembered it each time I rubbed my hands across my chest and felt the beestings I'd been left with after my partial mastectomy or happened to run a finger over my chest and felt the evidence of the PICC line that once rested comfortably on my right side. And it was these painful reminders that kept me singing this song. Since the day I discovered my breast cancer, I'd wanted one thing – to be a normal girl.

NORMAL GIRL, what do you say now?
We own the world, 'cause we not going away now
Wait on yourself 'cause you can figure your way out
Normal girl
Why do you, babe?

THE CLEAR WATER lost its clarity as I dipped the thin, lengthy brush into it, waiting as *Normal Girl* officially ended and the next song began to churn on the vinyl player. Days like this one, when the rain was heavy and the skyline resembled a screenshot of doom's door, were hated by many and loved by few. I was one of the few that awaited the gloom. It was when my creativity reached its peak.

Before striking the canvas with the honey-colored mixture coating my newly dipped brush, the prayer plant that was desperately attempting to unfurl it's new growth that had sprouted over the last few weeks caught my attention. A faint smile creased the corners of my mouth extending to the very ends of my eyes. Removing the brush from my hand completely, I laid it on the edge of my pallet and uncurled my legs from beneath me. After stretching to reach my full potential, I protracted my long arms into the air as a grunt left my lips.

"Ummmm," a slight hum followed.

With my indoor plant oasis being the center of my entire world, in addition to my artistry, their care was my top priority. The rain had been coming down hard and being that it was their care day, I knew that there was no better solution than rain water. It was natural – from the Earth, herself – and what they needed at the moment. My plant's care was another reason I loved rainy days. They'd sit out for hours at a time soaking up the goodness it had to offer. When they returned, I always noticed new growth sprouting right before my eyes.

Beep.

Beep.

Beep.

The cautioning sound of a large vehicle reversing registered in the background, hardly giving Sza a chance to make the runs that *Pretty Little Birds* required. Naturally, I gravitated to my open window that Mya had been begging me to put blinds up for and peered in the direction of the cautionary squeals. To my surprise, a large moving truck was being maneuvered into the driveway of the home next door to me.

It had been vacant since the day I'd officially inherited my great-grandparent's home. That was four years ago. Generational wealth was the motivation behind my family's moves. Each and every one of them. So, to discover that I'd been willed to receive their home when my great-grandfather passed – only a year after my great-grandmother earned her heavenly home – was no surprise. I was one out of three great grandchildren and we'd all been left a piece of land to build on or home to own.

Instead of selling or renting mine, I chose to live rent and mortgage free until I expired, too. There wasn't a single thing that I didn't love about my home, now. I'd left most of the original fixtures and the mainframe the same. However, I tore down some walls to create an open floorplan and updated the kitchen for a vintage and modern mashup. It was perfect.

My squinting eyes studied the scene, waiting patiently as the driver descended from the heightened truck and broke ground. A quick snap of the neck, checking out one side and then the other, he continued toward the drenched lawn in white sneakers that made me cringe after the first dip into the mud.

"Ewww."

Still, carelessly, he continued until he reached the FOR SALE sign that stuck out like a sore thumb in the middle of a neighborhood where every home was occupied with unchanging statuses for decades upon decades. When people came to this neighborhood, they never left. My great-grandparents had been here for over forty years. I planned to double their stay if the Lord allowed it.

Firmly gripping the sides of the metal post, he uprooted it from the soil and tucked it underneath his arm. The hoodie on his head that was tied at the neck restricted my view. And the dark skies due to rain wasn't much help, either. For the first time all day, I wished the rain would scatter and skies would brighten – temporarily, of course.

Curiosity nibbled on my skin and tapped at my feet. My previous revelation returned and the thought of my plants need for nature's gift was the perfect decoy to satisfy my inquisitiveness. Without second thought, I rushed into my kitchen and through the storage room where my wagon was folded into the corner. I fished it out before dragging it into my living room and placing my potted plants inside one by one. Eighteen. That's how many babies I had and I loved each one of them for a different reason.

Once they were all settled, I wheeled them out onto my porch, which wrapped around nearly my entire home. That was another aspect that I loved. From spring to fall, I spent many days out enjoying the spacious porch along with my art supplies and canvases. Sometimes it was large knitted sweaters and throws, coffee, tea, a book, or crafts. I'd find any excuse to get some fresh air, even if it was only as far as the porch that I wandered.

The wheels of the wagon stalled at the threshold of my frame, requiring a shove and a bit of hip to overcome the small obstacle. The unprotected end of the porch was their place of worship and where I was able to get a closer look at the thick specimen that I imagined I'd be calling neighbor.

Turn around. I encouraged inwardly, watching as he punched the code into the small box on the door and retrieved a key. The key let him into the home, but not before peeking over his shoulder – again, left and right. If I didn't know any better, one would think that either he had no business on this property or was on the run from something or someone. He was notable cautious and I'd only seen five minutes of him.

To my advantage, the request to turn around was granted by the paranoia that he obviously suffered from. Wrinkles crowned my forehead as a pang of concern traced the lining of my stomach and chest. Silently, I prayed that all was well in his world. At the realization that possibly all black men had an underlying reason to feel the same way he felt and take the same precautions as he did because of the hatred the world burdened them with, I sighed.

On a much lighter note and at the unfiltered glimpse of his handsome face, my heart lightened and stomach tightened. The hoodie he'd been wearing was removed at the doorframe as well as the shoes that he'd muddied on the way to remove the yard sign. During this time, I was able to see his features, uncompromised and in full bloom.

Ok. Wait. This isn't fair, I protested God's discipline. Putting a man next to me with the most chiseled cheeks, thickest frame, and ground coffee colored skin would be pure torture. Especially incorporating the fact that all the good men were taken and there was possibly a wife with a slew of children somewhere not too far behind. Had to be.

Enough, Sew. My thoughts were way ahead of me as I positioned the last plant near the table that they rested on when outside. Lifting them from the ground was one way to prevent bugs and critters from finding their way into the soil and nesting in my home. One last look across the lawn that separated our homes and I was blessed with the round, browns of Mr. Neighbor. Just as quick as he'd looked up, he'd looked off, removing a blaring cell from the pocket of his black sweats.

A second truck rounded the corner as I began my stroll back into the house to flip the vinyl that had been playing. This one, however, had a company name sprawled on the side. Two young men jumped out, immediately falling in line and climbing the back of the truck that was ready to be unloaded. I watched as they greeted the man who'd initially shown face, confirming what I'd already gathered. He was the homeowner. He was my new neighbor.

TWO

sew sidora

"ARE YOU UP?" Mya questioned, barging through the front door, half uninvited and half welcomed.

"If I wasn't?" I sighed, rubbing the sleep from my burning eyes.

"Then, I guess it wouldn't matter, because I'm here, now."

"Exactly," I groaned, "Don't you have like children

and a husband to tend to? Why are you here... and so early?"

"Actually, the girls are at school and my husband is gone to boss people around and do no real work of his own. It's just me... and you, now."

"Unfortunately."

"No. Not unfortunate. What's unfortunate is you neglecting to tell me about Mr. Neighbor! I know you, Sew. You're nosey and your ass probably found out the minute he stepped foot on the property. Why did I have to find out from my husband that someone bought the house next door to us? And, not to mention the fact that he's a brother and fine as fuck!"

"For that exact reason. You don't need to be lusting over a man when you have a husband," I reminded her, locking the door behind her and slamming my back against it. It was too early in the morning for her crap.

"Bitch, I'm married not disabled. I can look. As long as I don't touch. Now, imagine my surprise on my way over to your place and happen to run into the black God himself bringing linen and bags into his new home. Hell, I almost asked if he needed my help but in these pumps I knew it would look quite desperate."

"Mya? He's out there, now?" I rushed out, finally ridding myself of the sleepiness my body had been riddled with. Exhaustion seeped from my being as beads of energy crept from my toes to the tip of my head.

"Yes!" She chanted, waving her hands as if she was

scooting me along, knowing exactly where I was headed.

I scurried toward the window with pep in my step. Snooping wasn't exactly my forte but I was slightly intrigued from the small glimpse of my new neighbor that I'd been blessed with. Simply put, my interest was piqued. Not exactly for him, but with him. His history. His story and how he'd made it to my part of town. I wanted to know what had brought him here, and who would be accompanying him during his stay.

"Do you think he's gay?" Mya whispered as we stared out of the huge window – one of us on each side of it. Neither bold enough to stand in the middle where we'd be noticed.

"Mya! Does this man even look gay to you?" I hissed, shaking my head with a low rumble of laugher.

"Most of them don't. Shit. You have to be sure these days."

"Well, if he doesn't then how do you think I'd know?" I pointed out.

"Yeah," she shrugged and nodded, "You're right. I peeked over there last night to see if a wife or girlfriend would show face," she added.

Of course you did, I thought.

"But, no one showed up and there aren't any myste-rious cars on the street, either. So, you know what that means," she raised a brow and ended her question with her eyes trained on me.

"No, I don't, Mya, and why are you all up in that man's business? You really need something to do with your time instead of finding pretty heels to walk around the house in all day."

"Ma'am, I have a lot to do with my time. I have the girls three out of five days a week and that is saying enough. The two days that I get alone, I'm always going to get my heels out and prance around every minute they're gone if I want to. Hell, I'm in the house looking like an tired nanny. Anyway. That means that he is single and you will be taking him a welcome dish around dinner time, tonight," Mya stated as a matter of fact.

"No, I won't be. That man's relationship status has absolutely nothing to do with me," I combated as I removed myself from the window after realizing Mr. Neighbor wouldn't be coming back outside anytime soon.

Mya was right behind me, plopping her shoes off her feet to keep up with my swift steps. "Come ooooon, Sew. When are you going to let you hair down and let somebody love on you? I'm tired of you trying to cuddle with me when I come over."

Stopping dead in my tracks and causing her to run into my heels, I hissed, "I prefer dick, Mya. You have nothing to offer me but friendship."

"People have soulmates that aren't exactly sexual or from the opposite sex," she corrected, then chuckled.

"But with the way you be all up on me I wouldn't put it past you to be bumping pussies with a pretty woman one day."

"Please go away!" I walked off, unable to hold in my laugh. Mya didn't care what she said. Whatever came to mind came out of her mouth.

"No, but for real. You should. What's the problem with that? I'm sure he doesn't have his dishes and pots ready to go. His fridge probably isn't even stocked. You would just be helping out a neighbor," she reasoned as we reached the bathroom.

I grabbed my toothbrush after cutting on the light. "No, Mya. I'm not doing it."

"What is the problem? Why are you always so against meeting someone new?"

"What's the point, Mya?"

"What do you mean what's the point? The point is to fall in love. To be loved. To experience real love!"

"No. Not interested," I shut her down.

"I know exactly what it is, Sew, and you're not being fair to yourself. To your heart. You deserve more than you're willing to give yourself."

"All for what, Mya? To lose it all in the end? Break someone's heart unnecessarily? It's not worth it and I'm not that selfish."

"It's not being selfish, Sew. Not if you tell them upfront and let them choose to continue whatever you have for themselves. You're not even giving anyone a chance to decide. You're just making the decision for them."

"It's not that simple, Mya."

"It can be."

"But, it's not. Do you know how many people who are cured of cancer happen to get it again only a few years later. Sometimes the same kind, sometimes a totally different kind. You remember what I went through. I can't put anyone through that. It's torture. It's like living in hell every damn day you wake up!" Fuming on the inside, I jammed the toothbrush into my mouth and smeared the paste over my teeth as I brushed.

"I understand, babe, but you have to be a little more optimistic. I have faith that it won't return and I need you to have the same."

"Mya, no offense, but it's daisies and glitter in your world. It's dirt, mud, and grime over here in mine. I'm no optimist. I'm a realist and the real truth is that more than half of cured cancer patients later suffer from cancer. And, guess, what… they aren't so lucky the second time," I confirmed after spitting into the sink.

"Sew, please tell me, then, you think you can just live the rest of your life avoiding any resemblances of love and not hate yourself in the end if your cancer never showed? And, even if it did. So the fuck what? We will fight that bitch just like we did last time," she encouraged.

"You wouldn't understand and I would rather talk

about something else. I really don't feel like falling down the hole this morning."

"Fine, then we can talk about the dish you're taking over later tonight."

"No we can't because I'm not cooking that man anything," I shrugged, wiping my mouth after rinsing it. When I stepped back out into the hallway, Mya was on my heels. With her being so much shorter than me, it was comical listening to her attempts to keep up.

"Good, because I planned to do the cooking, anyway," she confirmed. I could hear the smirk on her face.

"Why are you here?" Plopping on the couch, I waited for her to do the same. Instead, she stood in front of me with her arms folded.

"Because if you don't want to fall in love and shit, at least you can get some dick from the damn man. I'm sure your vibrator's motor is nearly toast. Probably done wore the damn thing out, scoot over!" Before I was able to make room for her, she fell onto the couch and onto my legs.

"I'm not having sex with that man or no man, as a matter of fact. Please leave me alone. Every month it's the same conversation."

"Because when you're getting dicked down every night, you feel bad for any woman missing out on the Godly meat planted between a man's legs for her to enjoy. I, too, want your ass in the air and face in the mattress while you get your cheeks clapped from the back. I want that for you, friend, and you should, too." The seriousness on her face was repulsive.

"Mya," I pointed toward the door, "Get out!"

"Nope!"

THREE

sew sidora

GO HOME, Sew. I squeezed my lids until they pained.

Because, what the hell are you doing?

My thoughts ran rampant as I stood on my new neighbor's porch with the glass dish filled with broccoli and sausage casserole. Mya was adamant about the dish she cooked being a full meal, meat included. She'd also been adamant about me bringing it to our neighbor's home, which sat right in the middle of us. Her persuasion ended when she mentioned a shopping trip to our local craft store and groceries for the month – all on her.

While I wasn't the most social person, I never had an issue meeting or greeting new people. But, for some reason, I couldn't muster the audacity to rest my knuckles against the beautiful wooden door. I shifted my weight from one leg to the other for the millionth time as I sighed, lowly.

New art supplies. Free groceries, I mentally noted the luxuries this drop off would guarantee. Mya was downright evil for the things she managed to convince me of. I felt like a fallen fool as I lifted my arm, finally, and pushed forward to knock on Mr. Neighbor's door. Before they made contact, it swung open and the chiseled earthly God himself graced my twinkling eyes with his presence.

"Uh. Hi," was all I mustered before the lull of his baritone settled my aching heart.

---

umber nilsson

"MOVEMENT DETECTED AT *FRONT PORCH*," my security system chimed throughout my home as I sat in front of the television with a bowl of ramen noodles wrapped around my fork.

It was the same system I'd had installed at my other crib, and seemed to keep my stress at bay. Though far removed from my previous lifestyle, I still suffered from the cautioning behavior that led to my elevation. Deliberate, careful movement was the only movement I'd ever made and had granted me the benefits of early retirement and complete disassociation. I wished it granted me peace and serenity, but that was asking for too much. I'd always been a guarded nigga and just because I moved to the suburbs, I doubted it would change.

At the sound of the chirping, followed by the announcement of movement on my porch, I reached beneath the cushion of the temporary couch I was resting on and removed the .40 Glock. Carefully, I slid the bowl of noodles onto the table in front of me and stood to my feet. I located the safety bulb, and swung it in the opposite direction as I headed for the half-bedroom downstairs where my monitors became my eyes.

I studied them until I discovered the screen broadcasting my porch's surface. The system had only been installed for a few hours, the company opting to handle everything in one visit. It suited me well, because I had no intentions of allowing them into my home two days in a row.

Getting accustomed to the positions of the new cameras and the monitors their activity was displayed on would take some getting used to, but I would come around with time and not much of it, either. My safety was priority and knowing the ins and out of my security system could be the deciding factor between life and death in many situations. I knew that because it had been on several occasions for me.

Trained on the third monitor from right and second from bottom, I watched closely as the feminine figure fidgeted, possibly contemplating her next move. My gaze never faltered as she transferred her weight from one side of her body to the other, over and over. As she looked up and over, her features became more visible and her origin was able to be determined. She was my neighbor.

I'd caught a glimpse or two of her in the last twenty-four hours. Once on the porch as I was moving my things and another time in her window as she smeared paint on a white board. Not only did she not understand the importance of privacy, but it seemed as if she didn't respect it either. There was no way I should've been able to see into her home so easily. And, neither should she be willing to allow me too, either.

She turned, slightly stepping forward in the direction of my steps that led to my yard as if she was about to leave. Watching the movement, as simple as it was, caused a twinge of achiness in my chest which prompted my immediate reaction. Instead of continuing to watch the agonizing pivoting moment of her night, I decided to ease the worry lines that creased her beautiful face.

Besides, it was obvious that she had come bearing food. She struck me for one of the types who knew her way around the kitchen and probably enjoyed being the apart of the welcoming committee of the neighborhood. Maybe that was it or maybe it was the fact that I didn't mind seeing her expanded hips up close and personal that led me to my door. I noticed on the monitor that she was heading for my door, again, this time with her knuckles raised.

In a few steps, I was there. Before pulling it open, I stuffed my Glock into the back of my sweats where it tugged at the waistband. I cleared the ruggedness from my throat as I unlatched the hooks, removed the plank of wood, and unlocked the three deadbolts. And, finally, I was able to turn the knob to pull the door inward and put my neighbor out of her misery.

"Uh. Hi," she smiled nervously.

"What's up?" I tossed in her direction, watching as she came unglued before my eyes. It was as if my words had disturbed her more than her presence on my porch had done for me.

"I'm Sew. Sew Sidora and I live next door," she managed to make out, shaking her heads along with her thoughts I imagined. She recovered quickly. I liked that.

"I'm aware," I confirmed, "You should put some fucking blinds up on that window. A curtain, at least. I can see straight through your shit."

As a man whose job was to provide for and protect the women around me, I felt the need to extend that grace to my neighbor as well. Her features slacked as her face grew heavy with a sag. She wasn't expecting my bluntness, but neither was I expecting her beauty to be so damn alarming. I needed a distraction.

"I'm sorry," she began to retract, causing ruckus in my chest, "but maybe I caught you at a bad time. I'll just go home, now, where the plants aren't all that mean and the environment is pretty welcoming."

Shit, Um. I chastised, reminding myself to be a bit more considerate. A bit more courteous and a bit softer. Not every woman was the same and not every one of them preferred the intolerance that came with a man such as myself. It was obvious – off bat – that this was the case for my neighbor and if I didn't want to be at war or run her off, then I needed to get my shit in check.

"You're invited. Maybe I should've started by welcoming you inside and then telling you to put a curtain or something up," I eased, "But, either way, I was still telling you."

Stalling, she thought deeply before making her next move, "Welcome to the neighborhood," she sighed, "Again, I'm Sew. If you ever need anything, don't hesitate to ask."

Still sounding defeated, as if she'd lost a best friend, she turned and started for the steps. Naturally, I reached out to her, wrapping my fingers around her forearm and pulling her back onto my porch before she had the opportunity to take the last step. I'd gotten off on the wrong foot and the last thing I wanted was my neighbor to go to sleep assuming I was an asshole – or leave with the food she brought for me. I was certain the noodles I'd heated were cold and no good, now. She was literally my only hope at being fed, because I wasn't up for a late night run to any of the restaurants near.

"Aight. I apologize. I'm all in your fucking business and your curtains don't have shit to do with me. Let's forget that I even mentioned them. Maybe even try this again. You can knock without hesitation, I'll open with the same urgency, you'll introduce yourself, we will be all weird and shit, then you can leave me with whatever is smelling good in that damn pot of yours cause my stomach touching my back."

Instead of responding, her eyes followed the trail that connected my fingers with her arm. Upon recognition that I was still holding onto her, I released my grip and stepped back to give her the personal space that we all were entitled to. Visibly relieved, she looked up at me with a nod.

"There's no need. I appreciate you looking out for me, but I'm an adult who can handle her own."

"I get it," I nodded, still not feeling the lack of privacy. "What's in the bowl?"

"Broccoli, cheese, and sausage casserole," she shifted her weight, prompting me to reach out and remove the glass dish from her hands.

Though slightly, our fingers united, sending her eyes flying upward until they reached mine. A nervous chuckle seeped from her throat as her eyes began to glisten and crow's feet shaped the corners. I appreciated a woman who smiled with her eyes.

"I appreciate you," I admitted, meaning every fucking word.

After such a drastic life change, it was rewarding, seeing a woman of her essence. My world looked a lot different just months prior. Shit was blurry and I couldn't determine which way was which. Now out of the thick of things, the calm was welcomed and so was her softness. I could feel it from afar.

"Well, it wasn't all me. Actually, our neighbor, Mya, cooked it. I'm just the messenger since she couldn't bring it over herself."

"That works, too," a low grunt followed the statement as I felt my own smile creep onto my face.

"Well, I won't hold you up. I need to get ready for bed and I'd like for you to eat before this gets cold. I'm not a fan of reheated food. Soooo. It was nice meeting you, uh," she hesitated, unsure of what to call me.

"Umber," my name flowed easier than ever, "I'm Umber. It was nice meeting you, too."

"If you ever need anything, I'm only a few feet away."

"Same, Sew Sidora," I nodded, watching as she stepped off the porch for real this time and started for her yard.

Her flowy skirt caught the wind's precious gifts as it swayed with her wide hips. She wasn't a small girl by far. Thin, but not small. She stood at least five feet and six inches. While her top half was slinky, the bottom was heavily founded. She was shapely, even in the skirt that attempted to conceal her curves. Baby girl was thick like cold oatmeal hours after preparation.

As she reached the threshold of her door, she turned one final time and gave a wave. Still, I lingered on the porch making sure she was safe inside before stepping into my home. The kitchen seemed too far for reasoning, so I removed the fork that still had my noodles wrapped around it and dug into the large bowl she'd given me after removing the foil.

Damn, this shit hitting.

FOUR

sew&sidora

HE'S GOT to be insane! I yelled, inwardly, standing on my porch watching the crate that my neighbor had sat out near his trashcan. The garbage men would be by the following morning and I couldn't risk them picking up the contents without first having a look. I didn't care what time it was.

I'd seen Umber in passing for the last three days, neither of us having more than a head nod or smile for each other. However, I was wondering if I should knock on his door and ask for permission to view the items in the crates or take it upon myself and just go for it. *Well, they are trash, so that has to mean he doesn't want them anymore,* I reasoned. *Decent enough.*

Without second thought, I removed my phone from the pocket of my sweats and headed down the steps of my porch. I activated the flashlight as I made my way to the crate that he'd sat out. It wasn't pitch black, but it was after seven and the sky was dim enough. My vision was far from perfect so any assistance was welcomed.

"Heaven," I cooed liked a newborn who'd just realized milk was on the way as I kneeled over the vinyl records that sat lonely in the large crate.

There were plenty. At least thirty, give or take a few. I imagined the feeling I was filled with must've been the same one the miners must've had when they finally discovered diamonds. Coming so close to death made me appreciate the simpler things in life. Even things as simple as a box of trashed vinyl records that probably no longer worked. However, I planned to try every single one of them until I found out.

For a little over ten minutes, I sifted through the stack of classics. There were so many greats. I was excited just to save some money and receive second-hand records. As a faithful thrifter, it was something about receiving something that someone possibly once cherished that sat well with my heart. Nineteen. That's how many I decided to keep. Others were either broken or I simply had no interest in the artist's music.

"Please tell me one good reason you're digging through trash? If you're hungry, you could've just come over and asked for a few dollars or some food," Umber greeted me with his bluntness.

His dark skin aligned with the darkening sky, making it quite difficult to make him out completely as I stared up at him. He was half dressed, shirt missing and gray sweats imprinted by his lifelong friend. Swallowing the lump that formed in my throat upon recognizing the nice bulge, I lowered my eyes to the records in front of me.

"One man's trash is another's treasure," I reminded him.

"Yeah. I guess. Look, come wash up and grab something to eat. You fed me last week. It's only right that I return the favor," he insisted, waving me over to follow his steps.

"I told you I didn't cook that. Mya, our neighbor, did."

"Same difference. I can hear your stomach over here. Get up and come in."

He was leaving me no choice, so I decided to poke fun, "I hope you know how to cook, because I'd rather have an empty stomach than an upset stomach."

"Don't insult me. I know a little something. I'm not foreign to domestication. My mother was a single woman who worked hard. I was at home alone pretty often, caring for myself at a very young age. Seven, I think was the first time she left me home alone for a full work shift," he shared as I followed behind him with the records in my hand.

"It wasn't until I was a teenager that my parents left me home alone."

HIS HOME WAS IMMACULATE, even with it not being fully furnished. I'd been inside when it was completely empty and thought that it was a solid foundation and beautiful. However, I was reconsidering seeing the fixtures he'd added. It was stunning. Unlike most of the houses on the street, this one was built only a few years prior to my move. Approximately six to be accurate.

The people who originally lived on the plot had a house fire and it was too much damage to recover. So, they rebuilt a new home instead. It was like something from a magazine or movie. Very dreamy. Minimalistic. Luxury. One of the homes you'd often see the rich man or woman pull into with their Benz or Beamer. Umber, however, drove a Range.

"I'm still trying to figure out how you were able to score the exact wine that I absolutely love. Are you spying on me?" I sipped, giggling as I felt my buzz creeping up on me.

"I wouldn't call it spying when you're openly offering information with that big ass window you sit in front of. I've seen this bottle on the pane twice since I moved in. I figured if I was going to feed you then I'd may as well quench your thirst, too," he meddled.

"You just aren't going to get over the window, huh?"

"I'm not."

"Well, you should try because I'm not putting anything up there. I love staring out of it while I paint."

"And, what are you painting, now?" he asked.

"You," I admitted, unashamed.

"Me?"

"Unintentionally, you became my muse. I didn't notice until I was halfway through that it resembled you."

"Halfway through, huh?"

"Yes. It's not you exactly, but it was inspired by you. The features, the strength, the eyes, the lips, and that's pretty much as far as I've gotten so far. And, the skin, dark like night."

"Definitely has to have the skin," he nodded with a smile, proud of his deep tone. I admired his confidence.

"Definitely," I nodded in response, finding my tone drifting but my eyes planted on the skin we were both referring to.

Umber was a dream. I'd watched him, shamefully, from the window that he hated for the last four days and noticed he was without flaw. He was carved like a God, thick everything and the perfect height. He was around the three-hundred pound mark with about six feet five inches of meat and bones. While he was a large man, it didn't seem that he had an inch of fat on his body.

My girl parts began chattering, cheering for an eventful night that I simply couldn't offer. When my chest joined the party, I was aware that it was time to depart. My head was still in the game, holding on by a thread.

"You're beautiful," Umber cleared his throat.

The silence thickened the air, nearly suffocating me to death. I felt as if there wasn't an ounce of oxygen left for me to acquire. Surely, if I stayed any longer, I would succumb to death. I had to get out – and fast.

"I should get going," I sighed, placing my wine glass on the table. It was my second cup. Huge mistake. I should've stopped at the first.

"But you haven't finished your wine," he reminded me, nodding toward the glass in my hand.

"I'm aware. However, it's best that I leave, now."

"But, I want you to stay," he confessed, summoning my eyes, again.

"It's better that I leave, Umber," I tried, again, my stance weakening at the sound of his voice and the confession from his tongue.

"Better for who?" he questioned.

"Better for me… You. Both of us," I assured him.

"I'm a man that doesn't like to be spoken for. I'm capable of speaking for myself and believe me when I tell you that nothing – right now – would be better than having you stay a little while longer."

"I can't."

"You can, but you won't."

"Something like that," I nodded.

"Exactly like that."

"Well, that's what it is, Umber. I won't stay."

"I like you. I really do. As the days go by and the nights draw them to a close, I realize just how much more I like you. I can't remember a day or a moment that I found myself intrigued with the mere thought of any woman. But, since the day I saw your nosey ass peeking from that window as I pulled into this driveway for the first time, I've been wondering more about you.

"About your softness and how it was acquired. About your simplicity and how you discovered it. About your mind. About your thoughts. About your heart. About your good and about your bad. I've been busy as fuck, but I've been waiting since the night you left my porch for you to come back over. This time, because I invited you. And, this time, hoping you'd never want to leave because after spending the last hour with you… I simply don't want you to leave."

"It's not that simple, Umber. I've enjoyed dinner, everything was delicious. But, this is as far as it goes for me. I'm not in a position to…" I trailed off, knowing he'd never understand.

"I'm not in search of perfection."

"I'm not in search of anything."

"But, something has found you. Someone has found you. I've studied you and I haven't discovered anything that would hold you back or keep you from at least letting me get to know you on another level," he tried.

"I just can't, Umber."

"You won't," he corrected.

Nodding, I felt a pang in my chest. Even for it to beat was agonizing. With every pull and tug of the vessel, I found myself in pain. My lady parts had quieted, but my heart was screaming. Loud in my chest. Beating against it, demanding that I retract my statements.

"Fair enough," he concluded, accepting defeat well. "Feel free to take the glass and the rest of the bottle home with you."

Umber stood to his feet, crushing me in the process. He had dealt with my rejection gracefully, moving on as if it hadn't phased him a bit. I wasn't sure if I was more relieved or saddened but the moment I stood to my feet, I knew the latter. My heart crumbled with each step I took toward the door. I wanted, desperately, to recant and stay, but I knew that I couldn't. He didn't deserve the unfortunate possibilities that my future held. I wouldn't wish that type of pain on anyone.

"Thank you." We'd made it to the door when I finally found words, again.

"Na. Thank you for joining me. As stated before, if you ever need anything I'm right next door."

"Yeah. Same thing applies," I smiled, cradling the bottle in one hand and the cup in the other.

For a moment, there was an absence of movement and sounds from our mouths. There were only stares and baited breaths as we waited for whatever was to come. My eyelids sealed themselves involuntarily as I noticed Umber's face lower, closer to mine. So close that I could feel his breath on my face. Then, on my nose. I waited for the kiss I'd secretly been longing for. The one that united our lips and I could feel the softness I was sure his possessed, but it never came.

"You want me to kiss you, but I'm not," he whispered in my ear, "You've made it clear that you're not interested in a nigga. So, it's better if I kept my lips to myself. Better for ya know… the both of us. Because if I ever put them on you, you'd lose every sense of logic and before either of us can stop me it'll be your lowers lips that I'm sucking on. We both know that a face to sit on always turns into a dick to ride on but you're not ready for that, Sew."

"Umber," I rushed out through labored breaths. My panties were ruined. No good at all.

"Sew," he returned, stepping back and watching me succumb to the emotional flare that led to physical alterations, "You should be getting home."

I scurried from his porch, feeling a bit more intoxicated than I had been when we stepped onto it. His words left me dizzy. He'd casted a spell and I'd been dumb enough to fall victim to it. His bluntness didn't stop at the lack of privacy that I preferred. It went well beyond. He'd been upfront about everything he was feeling so when I found my way into my home I was wondering why I couldn't do the same.

Since our fingers touched when he removed the glass bowl from my hands, I'd been smitten. Wholly. He consumed my thoughts, daily. Hourly. By the minute. Every second, almost. He was inside of my head and tonight, I wanted him inside of my walls. Not the ones in my home, but the ones between my legs. For him, I wanted to break the rules I'd set for myself.

FIVE

sew sidora

FRIDAY NIGHTS WERE good for my soul. I spent them binging on the television that I never even powered on unless it was Friday and time for my shows. The old seasons of Girlfriends were circulating but I was more interested in the movie 365 days that Mya had mentioned a week ago. She and her husband had watched it and she'd sworn by it. With my homemade popcorn in hand, I snatched the blanket from the back of my couch and pulled it over my legs. My oversized tee wasn't enough to keep them warm, especially not with the ceiling fan swinging.

As I got comfortable, my eyes naturally gravitated toward my open window – which happened to be right in front of me. Umber was backing his vehicle into his yard with his music blasting. I watched as he removed himself, still bobbing his head. Just as mine naturally gravitated, his eyes did the same. For a moment's time, we stared at one another. Before things got awkward, I decided that at least one of us should make a move.

"Hi!" I yelled with a wave, knowing he'd hear me. My window was cracked, slightly.

Frustration covered his handsome features as he started for my home. My anxiety tripled by the time he'd reached my window. I wasn't sure what he was up to, but my curiosity had lodged itself in my throat in the form of thick air.

"Give me your phone," he spoke through the open window, reaching inside.

It wasn't until I was up and handing it to him like a fool that I realized I was half naked, "Don't tell me your phone is off!" I joked, deflecting.

"I don't rock like that. We both know that. I'm locking your number in and mine, too, since you continue to put your life in danger. I wouldn't be able to live with myself if I let anything happen to you. Not only is this window wide fucking open, but you've got it raised, too. I don't know what type of shit you're on."

"I'm sure you were given the stats before you decided on your forever home. The police is almost never called to Channing Willow. The crime rate is practically nonexistent. Nothing is going to happen to me. I just happen to love nature and to let it in every now and then."

"Yeah, whatever. I'm from Dooley and I know shit can pop off even where you least expect it."

I didn't have a lock code on my phone, so Umber was able to call his cell without assistance. It rang before he hung up and handed mine back. He was obviously disgusted with my choices, but he'd be just fine.

"I'll be sure to call if someone is in here killing me," I joked.

"That shit ain't funny, Sew," he barked. "Have a goodnight and enjoy your popcorn and movie." His last few words came out as mumbled grunts because he was so busy pushing the window down until it connected with the pane.

"Are you serious right now?" I tossed my hands up in the air in total disbelief.

"Dead serious. Goodnight, Sew."

With a shake of my head, I returned to the comfort of my couch and underneath the warmth of my blanket. I'd possibly opt for a thinner one soon being that Umber had taken it upon himself to shut my window.

ALMOST AN HOUR into the movie and I understood exactly why Mya had suggested it. Massimo was everything. According to logic, I was possibly insane for thinking that he wasn't wrong for kidnapping his partner and making her fall in love with him, but I found a man of persistence to be attractive. His forcefulness and way with her had my lady parts thumping.

By the time she caressed his dick with her lips after denying him for so long, I could no longer contain my wandering eyes. The light to a bedroom upstairs in Umber's home caught my attention. His vivid structure appeared in the midst of the slightly opened blinds. While his privacy was still intact, I could make out every part of him and see bits and pieces of his skin through the small lines between the openness.

umber nilsson

SEW SIDORA. She'd had my head spinning since the day I noticed her peeking out of her window. The same fucking window I was watching her watch me from. With the remote that controlled nearly everything in my bedroom, I widened the blinds so that her curiosity wouldn't kill her. Completely oblivious to my knowledge of her snooping, I watched Sew removed the cover from her legs and gap them.

My window stretched from the ceiling to the floor. While hers was huge, my sight was restricted in addition, giving me a limited view. Recalling each camera and my security system, I considered the one camera that focused on the side of my house that was next to hers. I could change the direction remotely, which is exactly what I did. It was only fair.

At the site of her panties – pulled to the side – I slid the briefs I'd just put on down past my ass. Still in bed, I watched as she touched herself – encouraging the thoughts I'd acquired to do the same. The second my hand wrapped around my dick, Sew's head fell backward and mouth fell open. I would've paid any amount of my savings to hear the moans that escaped as she avoided the intensity of the pleasure staring at my dick as I stroked it.

The Vaseline was never very far. As a man who was, now, more cautious than ever about where he buried his bone, the only action I was afforded was that of my own. I removed it from the cubby of my headboard and slathered it on my dick, greasing it really good. The slipperiness allowed me to stroke my shit freely, still watching the phone of my camera as Sew did the same. Only now, her eyes were trained on my window as she watched me from afar. Suddenly, my privacy wasn't a factor and I was violating every rule that I'd put in place to maintain it. Sew was a bad fucking influence.

I gazed at the small screen, gripping my dick in my hand and squeezing slightly each time I reached the tip of it. Sew could hardly sit still as she stroked her nub. The minute she removed her fingers, slid them into her mouth, and then placed them at her opening, I almost lost all self-control.

Sexy as fuck. My chest tightened as I witnessed her maneuver her insides without my help. Both jealous and intrigued, I sped my movement. I wouldn't even last another two minutes. Neither would Sew, obviously, because she'd began bucking her hips and lifting from the couch.

"Fuck," I hissed underneath my breath, sensing that the end was near. "Fuck!"

I became undone as I watched Sew's juices pour from her pussy. She was a squirter. I'd never in my forty years of living been involved with a woman who had the capability. So, seeing her ejaculate so easily – and unassisted – caused my semen to jump from my dick. In the sky and then down onto my thighs and briefs, it rained.

"Shit. Fuck," I continued massaging it until I had nothing left to offer.

Without a single lapse in time, I redirected the camera so that it was no longer focused on her window. Then, I accessed my call log and pulled her contact to message. At this point, I didn't give a fuck what her mouth said. I'd seen what her pussy could do at the mere thought of me and how her body reacted to me when I was around. Frankly, that was enough and I had no intentions of halting my pursuit, even if I'd let her think she'd gotten away for a few days.

SoSo, I had labelled her contact with a flower next to it. Her house was full of them, another fact I discovered through her window. I'd never be okay with that damn window and I'd make sure I let her know each time I got the chance. Just as easy as I'd seen her little freak show, someone else could've as well.

Goodnight, I sent, watching her jump from the position she was in when she felt the vibration or heard the chime.

She stared at the phone for a few seconds with her hand to her chest, the same hand she'd been digging in her guts with. ***Who is this?*** She replied.

Flattering, I responded, finally closing my blinds and capturing her attention. She stared straight up at me as I stood in the window with a gap in the blinds that my finger had made. ***Close your legs***.

Immediately, she jumped up from her position and gave me the finger. ***Are you watching me?***

***Your window is wide open, Sew. Everyone on the
block is probably watching you.*** I reminded her.

Goodnight, Umber.

Goodnight, Sew.

Of course she didn't want to hear about that damn
window. Chuckling, I tossed my phone on the bed and
headed for the shower, again. I needed get that damn
girl off my brain.

sew sidora

GOOD MORNING.

I rolled over to a chiming cell. Without checking it, I already knew who it was and what it read. For the last two days, Umber had been sure to send good morning and goodnight texts. It was agonizingly cute. Yesterday, he'd even texted at lunch and asked if I'd eaten anything. I'd just scarfed a salad down, which he seemed to be bombed about. I, however, was delighted. The last thing I wanted was to be around Umber.

The other night had proven that I was no longer to

be trusted around him. The way my lady parts responded to his manhood and the obstructed view of it, I knew that it was best if I kept my distance. I was doing a pretty good job of it, but his constant reminders of the care he wanted to take of me in the form of texts were wearing me all the way down.

There's something on your porch. Step outside. He sent immediately after.

And, there was. There were two new snake plants with potters and soil for repotting. I didn't even get to brush my teeth or wash my face before I ran out to see what was waiting for me. The realization that I was looking a hot mess didn't come until I heard Umber clearing his throat.

"I take that as you like them? Whatever the fuck they are," he stood at the last step.

"Yes. I love them. Thank you."

"Are they good enough to win me a lunch date with their new mom?" he tried with the prettiest smile stretching his face.

"Sorry, I can't," I admitted. "I have a commissioned project that I received some time ago and is due in the next 24 hours. I will be working through lunch."

"Fair enough. My day is pretty fucking empty, so if you need anything then holler at me."

"I will," I nodded. "Thank you, again."

"No need. Go brush your teeth and shit. I can smell

your breath all the way over here," he chuckled into a closed fist.

"Get off my property, sir!"

WHEN LUNCH FINALLY ROLLED AROUND, I was miserable considering the fact that I'd rather be in bed than at my station finishing up the piece I'd been hired to create weeks prior. It was just like me to wait until I couldn't any longer before actually starting the project. Nevertheless, it was beautiful. The mother and daughter illustrations were my favorite.

My stomach protested my work ethic with low grumbles. I had skipped breakfast and would possibly be skipping launch. The natural Salt + Vinegar chips that I had been snacking on would simply have to work. I wasn't moving from my position or throwing my energy off. If I ate anything heavy, I'd fall asleep and there wasn't a drop of salad mix left from the large one I'd made yesterday.

Choosing not to care, I pushed through with promises of taking a break in an hour or two. My vinyl continued to stop after only about five tracks before it was necessary that I either flipped it over or replaced it with a new one. The mood was utterly blissful. As stressful as it was handling commissions with deadlines approaching, it was just as thrilling. I worked best under pressure. It was my core when it came to my creativity.

Tap.

Tap.

Two taps on my window startled me, causing me to retract my brush from the brown faces I was filling in to peek in its direction. A smile tugged at my lips and nearly split my heart in two simultaneously as I shook my head. While I couldn't see his handsome face, I was well aware of who the culprit behind the bag and poster was. It was Umber.

Can we come in? his board read in pretty decent writing.

Standing from my seated position, I rushed to the window and lifted it, slightly. "Yes. You two can come in," I referred to the *Baisleigh's House* bag and Umber, himself. "But, him first!"

Through the window, I pulled the bag inside and then shut it back down. Umber immediately tossed the large poster presentation he'd created and made his way to my front door. I hopped toward it in my messy overalls and top knot.

"Well, don't you look productive," Umber whisked past me, but not before planting a kiss on my forehead that completely paralyzed me.

He'd reached my living area while I waited at the door for all logic to return. As much as I appreciated the affection, it simply wasn't okay. I'd specifically admitted that I wasn't in a position to be seeing or taking anyone serious, yet Umber was completely shitting on my limitations. I didn't mind him coming by or bringing me food, but unsolicited kisses and things of that nature were simply unacceptable.

"You're going to stand at the door or you're going to come over here and eat?" he questioned, realizing I hadn't moved a muscle.

"Actually- I uh. I think it's best if you leave. I see now that having company while I work isn't the best idea."

"Sew. You serious right now?" he pondered, shaking his head and heading in my direction.

"Yeah. I just..." I couldn't think of what it was I needed to say.

"You just really not trying to fuck with me. And for what? What nigga fucked over you so tough that it has you warding off niggas who are really trying to do right by you? Grow with you? Kiss on you? Hug on you? Love on you? Treat you good and make sure you're good in life for the rest of your life? Tell me why the fuck I can't get my chance and I don't want to hear shit about you getting your shit together. I'm still getting my shit together, too, but that hasn't blinded me of my reality. I see two people that feel something for each other, even if it's the slightest of something, and nothing stopping them from exploring it. So, what's the issue, Sew?"

"Listen, I don't have to explain anything to you,

Umber. A no is no. I'm not sure why men feel so entitled to a woman simply because they're feeling her. I've
made it clear that we're not in search of the same thing.
In fact, I'm not searching for anything. Nobody hurt me,
Umber. That's not all that can happen to a woman that
turns her away from love. Life happens as well, okay?
And, since it happened to me I'm not too keen on the
idea of getting involved. You can either respect that or
never say a mumbling word to me again. The choice is
yours, but my mind is made up. I'm just not interested!"

My heart galloped in my chest as the words came
from my mouth. I meant most of them, but some I
didn't. I was interested, but I should've have been.
That's what mattered most. Umber said nothing as he
slid past me – sure not to touch any parts of my body –
and down the steps that led him to my walkway. Within
seconds, he was back on his side, in his truck, and
burning rubber out of the driveway. He was visibly
fuming and I was hurting – physically and emotionally.

SEVEN

sew sidora

I HATED depression so I did any and everything I could to avoid it each year. I'd been without it since I'd been cancer-free. However, for the last four days, I'd found myself falling deeper and deeper into an abyss. And, nothing I tried to bring myself out would help. Not even a girl's night with Mya that had happened the previous night and left me with a hangover this morning.

The sun had taken forever to lower, but darkness

finally found its way across the sky as I tilted the wine glass to my lips, sitting on my couch and watching the window for any signs of the man that was to blame for my sorrow. Yes, I'd brought this all upon myself, but he had no business moving in next to me. I'd been just fine on my own and avoiding contact with males. But, how the hell could I avoid my neighbor? We were bound to see one another at some point, no matter how much we tried to avoid one another. And, for the last two days, I'd been trying really hard.

Unfortunately, my success pushed me further down the hole of misery that I was trying hard to climb from. He was upset with me. I could tell. He didn't even look my way, through my window, or in my direction when he was out in the yard or getting out of his truck. He hadn't texted me or mentioned anything about my window. I'd left it wide open – raised almost all the way – hoping he'd find the audacity to fight me on it. But, he hadn't.

For the first time, I knew that taking Mya's advice was my best solution. Until I had the chance to explain myself and explain my situation with Umber, I'd be feeling like shit. I'd lied, completely. And though my mouth continued to tell him I wasn't interested, my actions showed otherwise. In a sense, I was misleading him and it wasn't fair to either of us.

Truth is, I was curious as to where things between us could go. I was interested in the lunch, breakfast, and dinner dates that he'd inquired about. I loved being around him and seeing his infectious smile. He didn't give me butterflies. I found myself lost in the most beautiful safari when he was around. The stomping of my chest and fluttering of my stomach were minute compared to the hammering of my lady parts, the roars of my mind, and the paralysis of my thoughts.

Not only did my mind tell me so, but my heart told me too. They agreed that Umber was good for me. Good for my soul. Good for my skin. Good for my body. Even if it didn't last forever or things didn't work out in our favor, he was a man that would've still been nice to have known intimately.

But there was the possibility of this nasty disease returning that kept me from exploring his crevices. The good, bad, and ugly. No matter how much of a front I put up, I was gravely scared. Scared that I wouldn't be able to do it, again, and come out victorious. Breast cancer had torn through me, mentally, emotionally, and physically.

Though it had been a long time, I was still tired from battling the disease for as long as I had. Exhausted. That's why I had time to smell the roses and paint extremely detailed pieces. I had nothing but time on my hands with the exhaustion I felt. I needed every second of every day to readjust, to recoup. It was a requirement, not an option.

And, I planned to tell him. I wanted to let him in. I

had to, to give him the opportunity to walk away from whatever it was he wanted with me. He had every right to and I was expecting him to once I gave him the statistics. But, still, anything was better than him being upset with me. My heart couldn't take it anymore.

It was going on eight and my wine glass was almost empty. I needed the liquid courage for the things I had to say to Umber. By the time eight-thirty rolled around, I would be good and toasted without a care in the world. Spilling my deepest, darkest fears wouldn't hurt as bad or sound as bad coming from my mouth.

So, instead of continuing to watch the window for any signs of him, I headed for the shower. If all else failed, we could at least tangle in the sheets before promising to keep our distance from one another. I hadn't forgotten the way his pole stood all those inches tall and neither had my lady parts.

EIGHT-THIRTY ROLLED AROUND SWIFTLY, the clock hitting it on the nose the minute I slid in the tube dress that I often wore around the house. It was rather fitting, but very comfortable. A piece that was able to be dressed up or down. Tonight, I choose a pair of Ugg slides, so I was dressing it down. Autumn had made its announcement and I'd heard it loud and clear.

I gathered my bearings and the piece that I'd finally

finished with Umber serving as my muse before stepping out of my door. Locking it didn't cross my mind, because I was only going next door. My return would be swift, I imagined, so I saved myself the trouble.

You've got this, Sew. I encouraged. Admitting that I had cancer and it had taken a toll on my body physically, mentally, and emotionally wasn't something that came easy for me. If I could, I'd avoid the conversation for life. Especially with the notion that it could return. In most patients, it did return. Some not so soon, and later in their golden years. Others, within a few years or within a few months.

Exhaling, I smoothed the lines of my dress and continued down my steps. I kept my eyes trained on the ground in front of me, willing myself forward. If I happened to look up, I knew I would run back to my comfort zone where I wasn't judged or frowned upon. My feelings were always taken into consideration and the silence was a blessing.

Fifty-two. Fifty-three. Fifty-four. I counted, finally reaching Umber's porch. Just as I raised my knuckles to knock on the door in front of me, I heard a door slam, followed by giggles and tiny chanting.

"Umi. Please calm down. I really hate all of that ruckus you're always making. Your dad's entire neighborhood can probably hear us!"

Simultaneously, Umber's door opened and he stepped out onto the porch beside me. My eyes found his, immediately. Regretful and remorseful, they were. And, then, there were my own. Prickling from the insides out.

"Sew," he extended his arms to me, but I stepped out of his reach. "Listen, I can explain."

"Goodnight, Umber," I hissed, slowly placing the painting at his feet. "And, please… please don't come after me."

I gathered as much of my pride that was left, stuck my head in the air and headed to my place. This time, I kept my eyes wide and chest firm. I couldn't help but admire the young boy who resembled his father as I cut through the grass to avoid making contact with he and the woman who seemed to be his mother. Her flustered appearance told me everything I needed to know. He was driving her insane. From Mya, I knew firsthand how exhausting motherhood could be.

It wasn't until I made it to the foyer and was able to shut my door did I deflate. My entire body. Everything caved. And, for the life of me I didn't understand why, but I began to cry. We'd talked. I'd shared things with Umber and he'd shared things with me over dinner. Him not mentioning the fact that he had a son, a family, simply didn't sit well with me.

It saddened me, if I was honest with myself. Though I gave him a hard time, deep down, I knew that I wanted something with him. And, I'd inherited the same trait other women had. The dreamer, who immediately imagined what forever looked like with their special person. Our forever included only children from my womb if we ever got that far. Had he cared enough to mention his son to me, my perfect picture wouldn't be so jagged.

Silly me, I concluded, sliding out of my dress and heading for my bedroom. I wasn't feeling much of anything at the moment. Not even awareness. I wanted to be in a sleep so deep that I'd need I siren to wake me.

I hated myself. I hated myself for breaking the rules. I hated myself for getting attached. I hated myself for having hope. I hated myself for falling. I hated myself for desiring. I hated myself for liking him. And, I hated myself for being so damn disappointed knowing that human were capable of almost anything – including mistakes.

EIGHT

umber nilsson

I WATCHED her quietly as she slept, waiting for the moment she opened her eyes. From the looks of her bedroom and the toll it had taken on my heart, it seemed as if she'd had a long night. There was used tissue paper all over her floor, closest to her bed. An empty bottle of her favorite wine on her nightstand. I despised the look of things. The last thing I wanted was for Sew to find out about Umi the way she had. It was unfortunate, on both of our ends.

My thoughts halted as I watched her stir in her sleep.

Her arms lifted above her head as she rolled over and slid the clock on her nightstand toward her. At the realization that it was after ten, she sprang from her pillows, sitting up straight in her bed. Her raw, unfiltered beauty was insane. You didn't see that shit too often.

"UMBER!" She screamed, clenching her bare chest. She was naked underneath her sheets, but until she felt better about things her nudity wasn't of my concern.

"Good morning," I greeted, calmly.

"Why are you in my house and how did you even get in?"

"The window," I pointed toward her living room. "How are you, Sew?"

"How do I fucking look?" she roared, sounding like an entirely different being. The chill, relaxed woman I'd grown to care for wasn't the same that I was speaking to.

"I know that you're upset, love."

"Love?" She chuckled sarcastically. "Umber, please just get out." Just as quick as she'd lost her composure, she'd regained it.

"I will, after I've explained myself."

"What can you explain, Umber? You have a son and a baby momma that you neglected to mention during your chase. That's about it. Nothing really to explain. Besides, I'm not interested. None of that matters to me."

"Then why were you there last night and why are there tissues all over your fucking room. Please don't play me for a fool, Sew. It's okay to care. It's okay to have feelings. I've got them motherfuckers, too, which is why I'm here right now."

"Well, that was last night, Umber. You being here this morning means nothing."

"You asked me not to come after you, so I didn't. And, I knew you were upset. I wanted you to calm down and get level-headed before we spoke."

"But, we never have to speak! You could've stayed on your side and I would've stayed on mine."

"Let's not do this, Sew. You cried your fucking eyes out last night and that's fucking with me. So, don't sit here and act like that shit didn't make you feel a way. It made me feel a fucking way."

"It should've. You're the one keeping secrets!"

"My son has never been a secret and if you'd let me explain I can give you the scoop. But, instead, you'd rather act like you don't fucking care when you're so close to tears right now that I can see them in your pretty eyes. But, I don't want you to cry, Sew."

Standing from the lounge chair in her room, I treaded toward her bed and sat down beside her. "I don't want you to cry and I don't want you feeling any type of sadness behind my shit. Truth is, Sew, we both have secrets. I'm willing to tell you mine but only if you're willing to tell me yours. You, too, have been hiding some shit and whatever it is I have a feeling it is the reason you're so scared to let me in but I'm not going to give up so damn easily."

"You have, already," she shook her head, the tears finally touching her face and my heart at the same time.

"I haven't. I just needed time to work on my own shit. The day that you told me to stop trying, I felt like shit. Thirty minutes after I left your house, I got a call from a strange number. I never answer numbers I don't know, but something told me to answer this one. I did and I'm so fucking happy I did. It was my son. Umi. I hadn't seen him since he was three months old, which was when I decided that fucking his mother just to see him would have to stop. She has bad fucking energy and I fucked up when I planted my seed in her. We've known each other all of our lives. We were just platonic. Fucking when time permitted or when we were bored. One of those nights led to a busted rubber and pregnancy.

"Our friendship was down the hill from there. Not to shade the mother of my child, because I'm not that type of nigga, but she's pure fucking hell. She wanted a relationship after discovering her pregnancy. I didn't, but I continued to do whatever, whenever just to be around and experience my first pregnancy and child's birth.

"After he reached three months, I cut all ties with our personal relations and wanted nothing more than to be there for my son. She wouldn't allow it. She literally picked her shit up and skipped town. Left with my son.

I've been searching for them for fifteen months to the day! It wasn't until her money got low and her family wouldn't help her out anymore that she finally decided to call me.

"As fucked up as the situation is, I'm so happy she did. That night... last night was the first time I've seen my son in over a year. He's a touchy subject for me. Still is. I know we shared shit with one another and opened about things that night that we connected over dinner, but tell me this, Sew," I paused, "How can I tell you about a son that I barely even know? My intentions were to tell you eventually, but I wasn't ready.

"For the last few days, I've been trying to come to terms with everything. I got them on the first flight to Channing and got her situated in a hotel. She asked for a few days to get her shit together and I gave her that because I needed time to clear my thoughts. The night that she came over, I begged her to bring Umi. I couldn't wait another fucking second to see my boy.

"Even now, he's there. Waiting for me to return. Sitting over there with my mom. She hasn't seen him in all this time, either. He doesn't even know who I am, Sew, and I'm his father. A good father, if his mother would allow me to be."

"I'm sorry," she cried harder, wrapping her arm around my neck and squeezing.

"There's no need to be sorry. And, there's no need to be crying."

"I'm not meaning to, but it's just so much," she whimpered, "with you and all that you have going on. And, then me."

"What about you?" I was more interested in.

"I feel like I'm feeling you so much. You make me so warm inside and I like that feeling. But, I'm scared of it, simultaneously."

"There's no need to be afraid, Sew. I'm not here to fuck over you. I can lay my shit all on the table right now if it means you agreeing to give a nigga a chance. I want it to be you and me. I like what that looks like. I love what that would feel like."

"Me, too," she nodded.

"Then, what are we waiting for?" I questioned, cupping her chin in my palm and pulling her face to mine.

Slowly, methodically, I squeezed her cheeks until her mouth opened and tongue was exposed. I sucked it into my mouth and nibbled on it before returning it to hers. The covers that she held closely to her body with the creases of her underarms, I began to pull down. Her resistance was alarming, causing me to stare deeper into the reason. Fear rested beneath the surface of her eyes, beckoning for my attention.

"What's the matter?" I needed to know.

"Everything. I had cancer, Umber," she began to cry, again. This time, uncontrollable sobs escaped her throat, ripping me into pieces.

"Whoa. Whoa. Why are you crying? You said that you had cancer. That means it's gone, right?"

She nodded.

"That's a good thing."

"My breasts were cut in half and the chances of it returning are pretty scary. Very high. I don't want you to fall for me and it returns and you're forced to live through hell with me. Or watch me die. Or, leave me because you can't take it."

"I refuse to speak that shit on your life but if it came to it, then we rocking the fuck out, Sew."

"You're just saying that now because you don't know what it's like."

"I know exactly what it's like. My mother is missing a breast, Sew. I know that shit first hand. It was me taking her to her appointments and sitting with her for hours while she received treatment. It was me who shaved her head for her before that shit took away her dignity. It was me who made decisions that she couldn't make for herself when it took a turn for the worst. Me. I know what it's like and I know that it is nothing when it comes to someone you love."

"Your mother," she stated in shock.

"My mother. And, she possess the same appreciation for the simplest shit just like you. I'm upset with myself that I hadn't figured this out sooner. It's something about being so close to death that changes you. She's never been the same. She's better. A better person, mother, and friend."

"The experience changes you. Humbles you."

"I agree, but what I won't agree to is you claiming shit for yourself that you shouldn't. You think we're walking around here worried about my mother's cancer coming back ten years from now? No. She's living. I even got a fucking stepdaddy out of the ordeal. You should do the same!"

"What? Get a stepdaddy?" Sew found comedy in my speech.

"No. You should fucking live," I palmed her face, bringing it closer to mine.

HIS KISSES WERE like bandages for all of the cuts and bruises that life had left me with. The shame I felt exposing the scars on my breasts had depleted as he slowly caressed them with his tongue while his rod poked at my opening, begging to be let inside. I spread myself for him, widely. I needed him to fill every crevice of me, leaving no room for fear or doubt.

"Uhhhh," he groaned as he parted the narrow space between my walls, making way for his thickness.

My nails created indentions in his back. He was encompassing, holding me tightly as he tore my ass to shreds on entry. I wanted to scream, but at twenty-nine years old I imagined it would make for teasing conversations later. So, I muffled several in the middle of his chest.

"Umber," I panted, once he'd reached rock bottom.

"Shhhhh," he begged. "Please don't call my name, yet. I won't be able to hold out."

Honoring his wish, I opted for slow, low moans as he began to slide in and out of me. The slipperiness of my lady allowed him to do so effortlessly. After a few strokes, I adjusted to his girth. It was a lot. Plenty. More than enough, but I accepted the challenge. Thick and long, his drove his lubricated dick into my mercilessly.

"Oh my," I panted, feeling the folds of my stomach tighten and my toes tingle. "Oh shit."

"Seeew," Umber groaned.

"Oh my God," I made out.

"That nigga can't save you," Umber flexed, lifting up and removing my feet from his waist and hiking them in the air.

He pushed them back as far as they would go and spread them even wider. I watched him watch himself disappear inside of me, time after time again. The pure adoration on his face led me to a special place, one where the stars aligned and the birds literally touched the sky. Unable to manage the clear view of his handsome face, scrunched from the pleasure he was receiving and extending, I closed my eyes as my peak reached *me*.

"Ummmmmmmberrrrr!" I screamed, unable to continue his granted wish.

"Fuck, Sew," he grunted, pulling himself from my honey pot and hurrying to place his set of lips onto my lower set.

As I came, he suckled my pearl like a precious fruit. My ass lifted from the bed and then slammed back down onto it repeatedly. I tried my hardest to push Umber away, knowing exactly what was next, but he refused. Moment later, my juices were extracted. They shot from me like water from a hydrant, wetting his entire face and the bed beneath us. Not missing a beat, Umber slid up my body until our faces touched and his dick was buried deep inside of me, again.

He immediately pulled me up and made his way off the side of the bed where I was hoisted into the air. My juiced caused the most beautiful smacking of my ass and his thighs as he handled me like a I only weighed a few pounds. In the air, he tossed me up and slammed me down on his dick repeatedly. By the time we reached the bed, again, I was on the verge of another orgasm.

Umber smacked my ass as he flipped me over and onto my stomach. I wasn't prepared for the hard, long dick that he slid into me from behind. Neither was I ready for the back shots that followed. He dug into me, putting a good pounding on my pussy that she'd still be recuperating from weeks from now. Nevertheless, I held my own and took everything he had to offer. As my second orgasm started at the tips of my toes, I heard Umber announce the same.

"I'm about to cum, Sew. I want you to catch this shit."

Immediately, I unraveled, raining all over his dick and forcing him out of my tunnel. His large hands grabbed my top knot and forced me to the ground before him. His rigidness slapped the side of my face as I fell to my knees. Before I was able to steady myself, it was being shoved into my mouth. Willingly, I accepted it into my warmth, feeling his bulging head ready to let go of all that he'd been holding onto. I sucked the tip of his dick as if my life depended on it, because it felt like it did. Second later, and I could feel his cum oozing down my throat.

"Shiiiiiiiiit," he panted.

EPILOGUE

LATER...

"HEY," his voice rang out through the slightly cracked window of my home.

"Hi," I returned, never removing my eyes from the canvas I was painting.

"You ate anything?"

Like clockwork for the last month and a half, Umber made his way to my window around the same time. He owned a moving company and was able to go about his day freely because his line of work relied on others hard work. Not his. He was able to pop into the office for an hour or two each day, but mostly ran all of his operations from his business phone. He'd confided in me, admitting that he was one half of a large cartel that he walked away from months prior to moving next door. He was a changed man according to the past life he revealed to me.

"I could eat," I admitted, finally giving him my eyes to hold.

"Then get dressed and come out front in the next ten minutes."

I was only wearing an oversized shirt, which happened to be his. He preferred me this way. Without panties and ready for him to slide in whenever he felt the urge. So many times, I'd watch him creep from his side and over to mine, climb through my window, and take was what already his before jetting off to let me finish my work.

"Where are we going?"

"We're meeting Umi and his mom at some spot she wants me to pick him up from."

"And, you can't do that alone? You sure you want me to join you?"

"Yeah. It's all good. She asked if it was okay if she

met you. I explained that I'm tired of keeping you two separated. You're ready to meet Umi and I'm ready to introduce him to you."

He was right. I was ready to meet him. While Umber reacquainted himself with his son, I watched from my window. They always seemed to be having to best time of their lives. Every Thursday through Sunday, Umi belonged to his father. He'd finally furnished his home completely, giving Umi his own room and bathroom, though he never slept anywhere but in Umber's arms. Some nights his mother would take him so that we were able to get some time together. On those nights, either he crept through my window or called me over.

Though things had started roughly, they were finally shaping up nicely. To hear that Umber had expressed his desires to connect his worlds was no surprise. He'd asked me a week prior if I was ready and I was. Umi seemed like so a good kid.

"And, she's comfortable with that?"

"She has no other choice, Sew. But, she'd like to meet you to see who her son will be around."

"Understandable."

"So, get dressed and meet me out front."

He knew it wouldn't take long. I didn't wear makeup or anything other than brow powder and mascara. My getup was always simple, too. With it being a bit nippy in the late Fall, I wore a thick, cropped hoodie and a pair of leggings. The two paired well with my Uggs and gray beanie. Umber was waiting outside in his truck when I stepped out. He greeted me with a kiss as I hopped into the truck and began buckling my seatbelt.

"You cute," he gassed me.

"Whatever. It's nothing. I literally have on nothing."

"And, you're still cute."

Umber didn't back down. He never did. Each time I'd reject the compliments that he'd give, he'd continue to follow up with them. If there was nothing else that I loved about him, it was his ability to reassure me along the way. Every day, he told me that I was pretty and showed me that I was loved.

His world stopped – completely – for me. When it came down to me, nothing beyond Umi mattered. It was us two, the biggest parts of his world. My gratitude was plentiful. I don't think he understood just how deep in ran. I was thankful. Grateful. Honored. In so many ways and for so many reasons.

"Stop gassing me, Umber," I chuckled, cheeks flushing an obvious shade a pink. He knew that he had me right where he wanted me.

"That's what I'm here for, love," he shrugged, reaching for the knob to hike the volume of his stereo. Mariah Carey's *You Will Always be My Baby* was blasting through the speakers as he leaned over and palmed my chin, singing along to the song. He was so corny and I loved every second of it. Seeing his large frame soften as he pitched a horrible tune, unable to keep up with the incredible vocals of Mariah, set my soul on fire.

This was it. This was the love that Mya had been wanting for me. The love that I'd secretly been wanting for myself. The love that my parents desired for me. The love that I deserved. And, while I never expected it to be for Mr. Neighbor, I wasn't complaining. In two months, he'd shown me what he was capable of. I couldn't wait to see what a lifetime with him would bring.

THE END.

CLUB GREY

Are you ready to be apart of Club Grey where you will receive exclusive updates, read unpublished stories that are ONLY for club members, get $$ off purchases and keep up with all things Grey Huffington?
Well, here's your chance.
Did I mention you can win prizes?

TEXT 'greyhuffington' to 900900

CHECK OUT MY LATEST RELEASES

Mr. Intentional

Situationship Series:
Syx and the City: Situationship Book One
Syx and the City: Situationship Book Two
Syx Thirty Sevyn
Syx Whole Weeks

Ready or Not Series:
The Sweetest Revenge
The Sweetest Redemption

Unearth Me

Leverage & Love Series:
Wilde & Reckless

Wilde & Relentless
Wilde & Restless

Half & Half

The Emancipation of Emoree

Sleigh

The Gifted

Unbreak Me
Unleash Me
Uncover Me

Memo

Just Wanna Mean the Most to You

As we Learn
As we Love

10,000 hours
Darke Hearts
lost one.

Made in United States
Orlando, FL
18 May 2024

46996177R00055